WE GIVE THANKS

WE GIVE

written by
Cynthia Rylant

illustrated by
Sergio Ruzzier

THANKS

Beach Lane Books • New York London Toronto Sydney New Delhi

We give thanks for mittens
and for coats and boots and hats.

We give thanks for yellow dogs
and yellow kitty cats.

We give thanks for apple trees
and bushes filled with roses.

We give thanks for nice warm soup
and fires to warm our toeses.

We give thanks for cousins
and for fathers and for mothers.

We give thanks for grandpas
and for sisters and for brothers.

Aunts and uncles,

neighbors too,

grandmas great and greater.

The mailman, the grocer,
and the nice Italian waiter.

We give thanks for sun and rain
and wind and sleet and snow.

We give thanks for bikes and skates
and cars that help us go.

We give thanks for beetles, bees,
and spotted ladybugs.

We give thanks for kisses,
and we give thanks for hugs.

We give thanks for plates and cups
and spoons and forks and ladles.

We give thanks for kitchens
and for food on kitchen tables.

Bless our nights and bless our days
and bless all those we meet.

We give thanks for *everything*,
and now . . .

it's time to EAT!